CHICKEN LITTLE

illustrated by Ruth Ruhman

 GOLDEN PRESS • NEW YORK
Western Publishing Company, Inc.
Racine, Wisconsin

© 1973 by Western Publishing Company, Inc.
All rights reserved. Produced in U.S.A.

1977 GOLDENCRAFT® Edition

One fine summer day, Chicken Little was scratch-
ing for food in the barnyard, near the orchard.

As she scratched and cheeped happily, a small red
apple fell from a tree and hit her—*plunk!*—right
on top of her head.

"Dear me!" she cried, rubbing her head. "The sky is falling! I must run and tell the king!" And away she ran, as fast as her little legs would go.

As Chicken Little hurried past the hen house, Henny Penny looked down from her roost and called, "Why are you hurrying so, Chicken Little?"

"Oh, Henny Penny, the sky is falling, and I am running to tell the king!"

"How do you know the sky is falling?" asked Henny Penny, much surprised.

"A piece of it hit me right on top of my poor little head!" Chicken Little cried, and she showed Henny Penny the bump on her head.

"How awful!" clucked Henny Penny. "I will come
with you to see the king."

Off they scurried, and soon they came upon
Cocky Locky, who was smoothing his beautiful
feathers.

"Oh, Cocky Locky," called Henny Penny, "the sky is falling, and a piece of it fell right on top of Chicken Little's poor little head! We are running to tell the king!"

"Dear me!" said Cocky Locky as Chicken Little showed him her bump. "I will come with you."

Clucking and crowing excitedly, they ran past the rusty old pump and out of the farmyard. Soon they came to the pond, where Ducky Lucky was ducking for his dinner.

"Why are you all in such a hurry?" quacked Ducky Lucky.

"The sky is falling, and we are going to tell the king!" Cocky Locky explained. Chicken Little showed Ducky Lucky where the piece of sky had hit her on her poor little head.

"Indeed the king *should* be told," said Ducky
Lucky, "and I shall come with you."

"Cheep-cheep" . . . "Cluck-cluck" . . . "Cock-a-doodle-doo" . . . "Quack-quack," they cried as they hurried off. "The sky is falling! We must run and tell the king!"

They made such a racket that they awoke Solomon, the wise old owl, from his midday nap.

"*Whoooo* says the sky is falling?" he hooted. "And *hooooow* do you know it is so?"

"Chicken Little told us," clucked Henny Penny.

"A piece of it hit me right on top of my poor little head," cheeped Chicken Little.

"*Shoooow* me where it happened," said Solomon, blinking his great, round eyes. Then they all followed Chicken Little back to the barnyard.

"This is where the piece of sky fell on my poor little head," peeped Chicken Little, pointing with one fluffy wing.

Each of the animals looked at the small red apple, which still lay right where it had fallen. Then they looked up at the apple tree. Finally, one by one, they walked away, until only Solomon the owl remained with Chicken Little.

Solomon blinked his eyes and said to Chicken Little, "*Doooo yoooou* see that apple that has fallen from the tree? If *yoooou* are a smart little chick, you will eat it up, before someone else does."

And that is just what Chicken Little did!

Favorite Fairy Tales

Little Mermaid

Retold by Rochelle Larkin   **Illustrated by Yvette Banek**

CREATIVE CHILD PRESS
is a registered trademark of Playmore Inc.,
Publishers and Waldman Publishing Corp., New York, N.Y.

Once upon a time, in a kingdom deep below the sea, lived a Little Mermaid. She was very happy there beneath the blue waters, with fish for friends and beautiful shells and sea flowers to play with.

The Little Mermaid was happy, but she was also very curious. She spent many hours swimming to the surface, looking at the sailing ships and the people on them.

Sometimes the Little Mermaid grew curious enough and bold enough to ask King Neptune, who ruled the sea kingdom, about people and their ways.

But the King always told her not to ask so many questions, especially about people and the place where they lived, called land.

That made her even more curious about a world that was not wet but dry, and where creatures walked on legs.

That was what she wondered about as she gazed at a ship one day, when suddenly a young man appeared on its deck. The Little Mermaid couldn't stop looking at him.

She swam closer and closer to the ship, trying to find out who he was.

At last someone approached the young man. It was a servant, and the Little Mermaid watched as he bowed and called the young man My Lord Frederic.

My Lord Frederic! The Little Mermaid thought it quite the most beautiful name she had ever heard.

Alone in her secret cave, the Little Mermaid sat and dreamed about My Lord Frederic. She knew she had to see him again. And not only see him, but talk with him, and walk with him.

The Little Mermaid flicked her tail sadly. Once she had been proud of that tail, shiny and beautiful and strong enough to help her swim the deepest oceans. But now she only wished she could walk someday with the handsome stranger on the ship.

King Neptune was angrier than the Little Mermaid had ever seen him when she went to ask for his help.

"Stay in your place," the mighty King roared.

But the Little Mermaid begged and pleaded. At last the King gave in.

It wasn't going to be easy. First she had to find My Lord Frederic. The Little Mermaid swam all along the ocean crest, back to where she had first seen the ship.

At last she saw it! But as the Little Mermaid came close, a terrible storm broke out. Thunder and lightning made the ocean roar, and the big ship looked very small as it tossed about on the enormous waves.

Even the Little Mermaid, who had seen many storms at sea, was frightened.

A great bolt of lightning tore the ship in half. A mighty wave tossed My Lord Frederic into the air and set him down on a tiny island.

The Little Mermaid swam faster than she had ever done in her life.

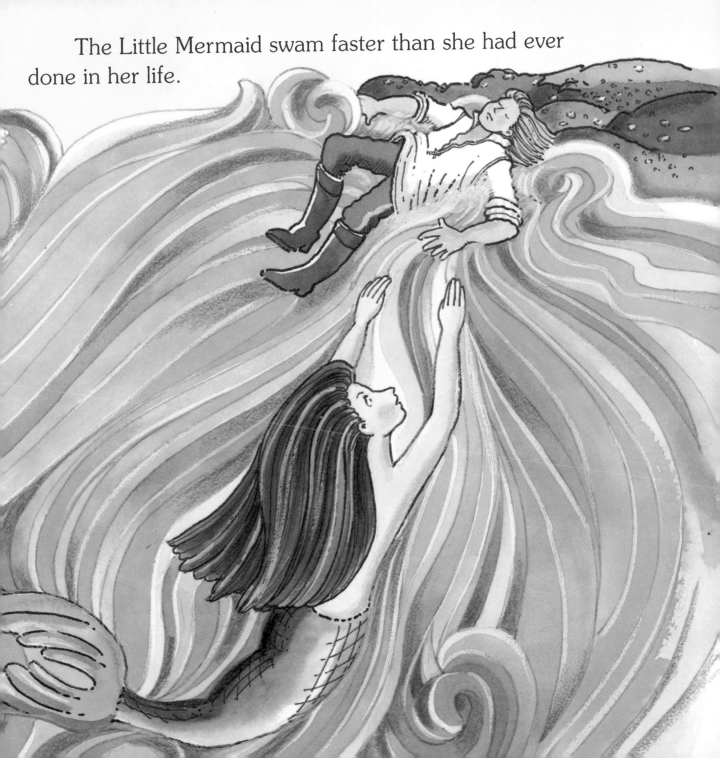

My Lord Frederic lay stretched out on the sand. He was very still. The Little Mermaid watched over him, fearful that she had found him, but too late.

Suddenly, he stirred. He opened his eyes and saw the beautiful Little Mermaid.

"Are you real, or am I dreaming?" he asked, rubbing his eyes. "Or are you an angel?"

The Little Mermaid laughed. "No, I am not an angel," she said. "I'm as real as you are."

She knew now that King Neptune had
caused the storm that brought them together on the little island,
and that all of the others on the ship were safe somewhere too.

"I'm a mermaid," she told My Lord Frederic. "I live in the ocean as you live on land."

"Now we must learn to live in both places," My Lord Frederic declared, "because I will never leave your side, not ever."

And they did learn to live in each other's ways, and so they were at home everywhere in the world, and lived happily ever after.